ONE
IS A FEAST FOR MOUSE
A Thanksgiving Tale

by **Judy Cox**

illustrated by
Jeffrey Ebbeler

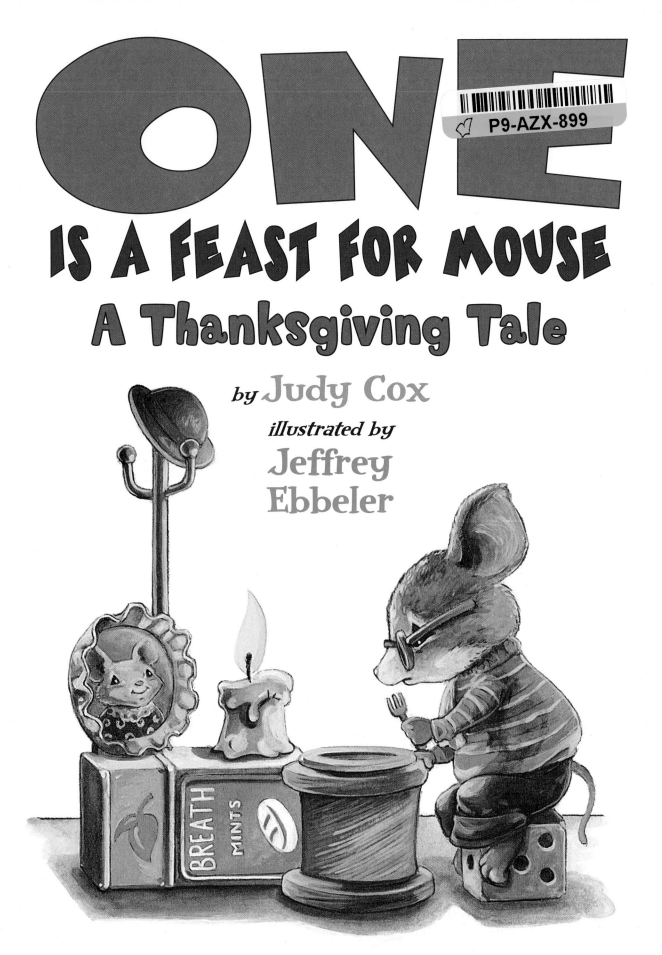

Holiday House / New York

To Mom and Dad
J.C.

For Kiera, Shannon, and James
J.E.

Text copyright © 2008 by Judy Cox
Illustrations copyright © 2008 by Jeffrey Ebbeler
All Rights Reserved
Printed in the United States of America
The text typeface is Cheese And Crackers.
The paintings were made with acrylic paint, pastels,
and colored pencils on paper.
www.holidayhouse.com

 3 5 7 9 10 8 6 4

Library of Congress Cataloging-in-Publication Data
Cox, Judy.
One is a feast for Mouse: a Thanksgiving tale / by Judy Cox ;
illustrated by Jeffrey Ebbeler. – 1st ed.
p. cm.
Summary: On Thanksgiving Day while everyone
naps, Mouse spots one pea, a perfect feast,
but he cannot help adding all of the
fixings–until Cat spots him.
ISBN 978-0-8234-1977-7 (hardcover)
ISBN 978-0-8234-2231-9 (pbk)
[1. Mice–Fiction. 2. Cats–Fiction.
3. Greed–Fiction. 4. Thanksgiving Day–Fiction.]
I. Ebbeler, Jeffrey, ill. II. Title.
PZ7.C83835On 2008
[E]–dc22
2007013972

After Thanksgiving
dinner Mouse crept out
of his hidey-hole and
looked around.

The house was quiet. Dad snoozed in his chair with his book. Mom dozed in front of the TV. Outside, the kids played football in the crisp yellow leaves. Cat curled up by the fire. He yawned and stretched his stripy tail. Then he closed his greeny eyes and went to sleep.

Mouse scampered up the tablecloth. Thanksgiving leftovers were still on the table. So much to eat!

Mouse saw a teensy-tiny, toothsome, green pea all by itself under a plate. Give thanks, he thought. One will be a feast for me.

Mouse rolled the pea across the tablecloth to take it back to his hidey-hole.

But his eyes were bigger than his stomach. He saw six leftover cranberries, glowing like rubies on a silver saucer. "I'll just take one," he said to himself. "One is a feast for me." He balanced one cranberry on top of the pea and started once again across the table to his hidey-hole.

Just then he saw three olives, black and
shiny, in a dish. I'll just take one, he thought.
One is a feast for me.

He put the olive on top of the cranberry
on top of the pea and carried the tidbits across
the table.

Then he saw the carrot sticks, crunchy and munchy and orange.

I'll just take one, he thought. One is a feast for me. He stuck one carrot stick into the hole in the olive, balanced both on top of the cranberry on top of the pea, and started back to his hidey-hole.

Then he saw the mashed potatoes. Mouse potatoes! There was just one scoop left on the plate. I'll just take the plate, Mouse thought. What a feast I will have! He balanced the plate of potatoes on top of the carrot stick in the hole in the olive on top of the cranberry on top of the pea. Mouse started off across the table.

Then he saw the gravy,
brown and luscious, in the silver
gravy boat. Gravy for the mouse potatoes,
he thought. I must have that for my feast!
And he balanced the gravy boat on top of
the mashed potatoes on top of the carrot
stick stuck in the olive on top of the
cranberry on top of the pea. And he
started off. . . .

But then he spotted the pumpkin pie!
One slice of pie, brown and dimpled, with a collar
of fluffy cream.

So he balanced the pie
on top of the gravy boat
on top of the mashed
potatoes on top of the
carrot stick stuck in
the hole in the olive...

on top of the
cranberry on
top of the pea,
and he started off
across the table.

The pie slid, but Mouse
caught it just in time. Mouse
bobbed and bobbled across
the tablecloth on the way to his
hidey-hole for his Thanksgiving
feast. He didn't see Cat
creeping, creeping closer
and closer.

But Mouse saw the turkey! Brown and juicy, surrounded with parsley. Much was gone, but there was enough left for a mouse feast—or even two! I'll just add that, thought Mouse. And he carefully placed the turkey platter on the very top of his pile. On top of the pie on top of the gravy on top of the mashed potatoes on top of the carrot stick stuck in the hole in the olive on top of the cranberry on top of the pea.

He started off across the table to his hidey-hole. And there, at the table's edge, he met **Cat**, greedy eyed and hungry, clawing up the table on the tablecloth.

Mouse skidded to a stop. The turkey wibbled and wobbled, slid and slipped. Mouse danced to keep his feast balanced, pirouetted like a ballerina, juggled like a platter-spinner!

But off slid the turkey! WHOOSH! With a PLOP! Landing smack on Cat.

Down crashed the pumpkin pie and the boat with the gravy. Down crashed the mashed potatoes with a clatter that woke Mom! Down fell the carrot stick, still impaled in the olive! Down went the cranberry, which rolled, leaving a red track across the tablecloth! Down went the pea, all catter-whumpus off the table, rolling onto the floor. Off scampered Mouse, quick as a bandit, back to his hidey-hole ahead of Cat!

He huddled in his hidey-
hole. His heart pitter-
pattered. He peered out.
Down came the broom on
the stripy, greeny-eyed cat.
"Bad kitty!" shouted Mom.
"Outside!" And she swept
the cat out the door.
Mouse looked around,
whiskers trembling with
fright. No Thanksgiving
feast for me, he thought.
Just then he spotted,
glowing in the corner . . .

. . . one teensy-tiny, round and toothsome, green and luscious pea.

"Give thanks! One is a feast for me!"